Editors: Ann Redpath, Etienne Delessert
Art Director: Rita Marshall
Publisher: George R. Peterson, Jr.

Copyright © 1984 Creative Education, Inc., 123 S. Broad Street,
Mankato, Minnesota 56001, USA. American Edition.
Copyright © 1984 Grasset & Fasquelle, Paris – Editions 24 Heures, Lausanne. French Edition.
International copyrights reserved in all countries.

Library of Congress Catalog Card No.: 83-71187
Grimm, Jakob and Wilhelm; Three Languages
Mankato, MN: Creative Education, Inc.; 32 pages. ISBN: 0-87191-940-0

Color separations by Photolitho A.G., Gossau/Zurich
Printed in Switzerland by Imprimeries Réunies S.A. Lausanne.

THE
THREE
LANGUAGES

JAKOB & WILHELM GRIMM
illustrated by
IVAN CHERMAYEFF

CREATIVE EDUCATION

THERE lived in Switzerland an old Count, who had an only son; but the son was very stupid, and could learn nothing. So his father said to him:

"Listen to me, my son. I can get nothing into your head, try as hard as I may. You must go away from here. I will send you to a distinguished professor for one year."

At the end of the year he came home again, and his father asked:

"Now, my son, what have you learned?"

"Father, I have learned the language of dogs."

"Mercy on us!" cried his father, "is that all you have learned? I will send you away again to another professor in a different town."

The youth was taken there, and remained with this professor for one more year. When he came back his father asked him again:

"Now, my son, what have you learned?"

He answered:

"I have learned the language of birds."

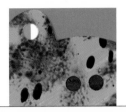

Then the father flew into a rage, and said:

"Oh, you hopeless creature, have you been spending all this precious time and learned nothing? Aren't you ashamed to come into my presence? I will send you to a third professor, but if you learn nothing this time, I will not be your father any longer."

The son stayed with the third professor for another year, and when he came home again, his father asked:

"Now, my son, what have you learned?"

He answered:

"My dear father, this year I have learned the language of frogs."

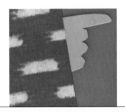

Thereupon his father was filled with anger, and said to his servants:

"This creature is my son no longer. I turn him out of the house and command you to lead him into the forest and take his life."

They took him to the forest, but when the time came to kill him, they took pity on him, and let him go. Then they cut out the eyes and tongue of a fawn, in order that they might take back proofs to the old Count.

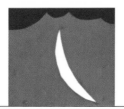

The youth wandered about, and at length came to a castle, where he begged for a night's lodging.

"Very well," said the Lord of the castle. "If you want to spend the night down there in the old tower, you may; but I warn you that it will be at the risk of your life, for it is full of savage dogs. They bark and howl without ceasing, and at certain hours they must have a man thrown to them. Then they devour him at once."

The whole neighborhood was distressed by this menace, but no one could do anything to remedy it. But the youth was not a bit afraid, and said:

"Just let me go down to these barking dogs with something for them to eat. Then they won't do me any harm."

So they gave him some food for the savage dogs, and took him down to the tower.

The dogs did not bark at him when he entered, but ran round him wagging their tails in a most friendly manner. They ate the food he gave them, and did not so much as touch a hair of his head.

The next morning, to the surprise of every one, he made his appearance again, and said to the Lord of the castle:

"The dogs have revealed to me in their own language why they live there and bring misery to the country. They are enchanted and obliged to guard a great treasure which is hidden under the tower. And they will not rest until it has been dug up. I have also learned from the dogs how this task is to be done.

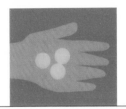

Everyone who heard this was delighted, and the Lord of the castle said he would adopt him as a son if he accomplished the task successfully. He went down to the tower again, and set to work. He accomplished his task, and brought out a chest full of gold. The howling of the savage dogs was from that time forward heard no more. They entirely disappeared, and the country was delivered from the terrible affliction.

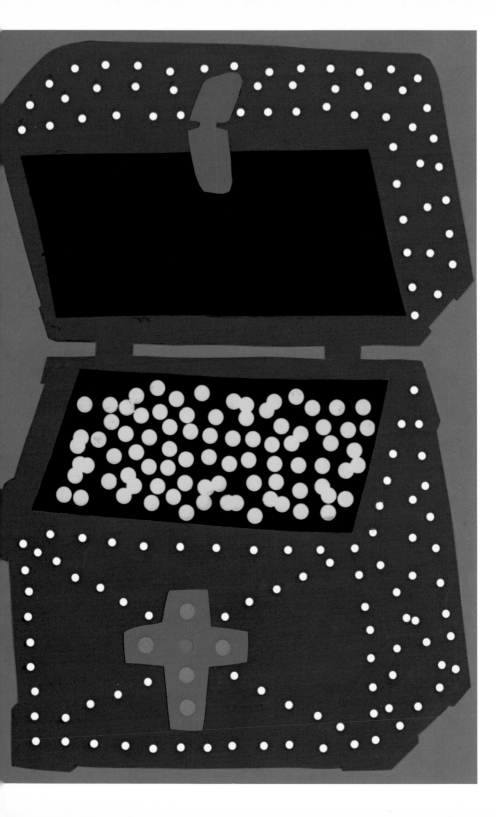

After a time, the young Count took it into his head to go to Rome. On the way he passed a swamp, in which a number of frogs were croaking. He listened, and when he heard what they were saying he became quite pensive and sad.

At last he reached Rome, at a moment when the Pope had just died, and there was great doubt among the cardinals about whom they ought to name as his successor. They agreed at last that the man to whom some divine miracle should occur ought to be chosen as Pope. Just as they had come to this decision, the young Count entered the church, and suddenly two snow-white doves flew down and alighted on his shoulders.

The clergy recognized in this the sign from Heaven, and asked him on the spot whether he would be Pope.

He was undecided, and knew not whether he was worthy of the post; but the Doves told him that he might accept, and at last he said "Yes."

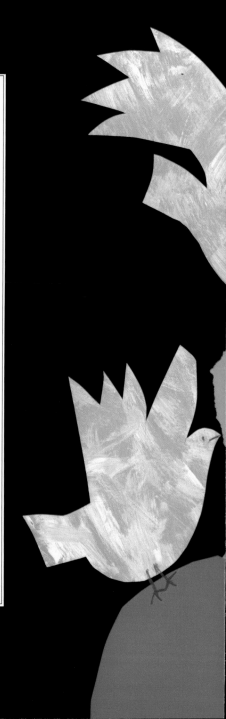

   Immediately he was anointed
and consecrated. The disturb-
ing news he had heard from
the frogs had indeed come to
pass. He became the Pope.
   Then he had to chant mass,
and did not know one word
of it. But the two doves sat upon
his shoulders and whispered it
to him.